THE
GLERP

Published by Silver Press, an imprint of Silver Burdett Press,
A Division of Simon & Schuster
299 Jefferson Road, Parsippany, NJ 07054
Printed in the United States of America

Library of Congress Cataloging-in-Publication Data
McPhail, David M.

The Glerp/by David M. McPhail: illustrated by David M. McPhail. p. cm.
Summary: At the expense of his health, the strolling Glerp
swallows everyone who gets in his way.

[1. Animals–Fiction.] I. Title.
PZ7.M4788184Gl 1995
[E]–dc20 94-20298 CIP AC

10 9 8 7 6 5 4 3 ISBN 0-382-24668-3 (LSB)
10 9 8 7 6 5 4 3 2 ISBN 0-382-24669-1 (JHC)
10 9 8 7 6 5 4 3 2 ISBN 0-382-24670-5 (S/C)

written and illustrated by
David McPhail

SILVER PRESS
Parsippany, New Jersey

This is a GLERP. “Glerp!”
A GLERP eats anything.

One night the GLERP went for a walk.
"If anything gets in my way, I'll eat it!"
said the GLERP. "Glerp!"

The GLERP was going out when an ant walked by.

“Glerp!” went the GLERP.

Poor ant.

A mouse stopped to ask which way to go.

“Glerp!” went the GLERP.

Poor mouse.

The GLERP saw a dog with a bone.

“Glerp!” went the GLERP.

Poor dog.

Then the GLERP met a lion. The lion growled at the GLERP.

“Glerp!” went the GLERP.

Poor lion.

The GLERP was much bigger now, and he was very ill. The things he had eaten were jumping around and having a wonderful time.

The GLERP walked on and met a cow.

The cow went “Moo.”

The GLERP went "Glerp!"

Poor cow.

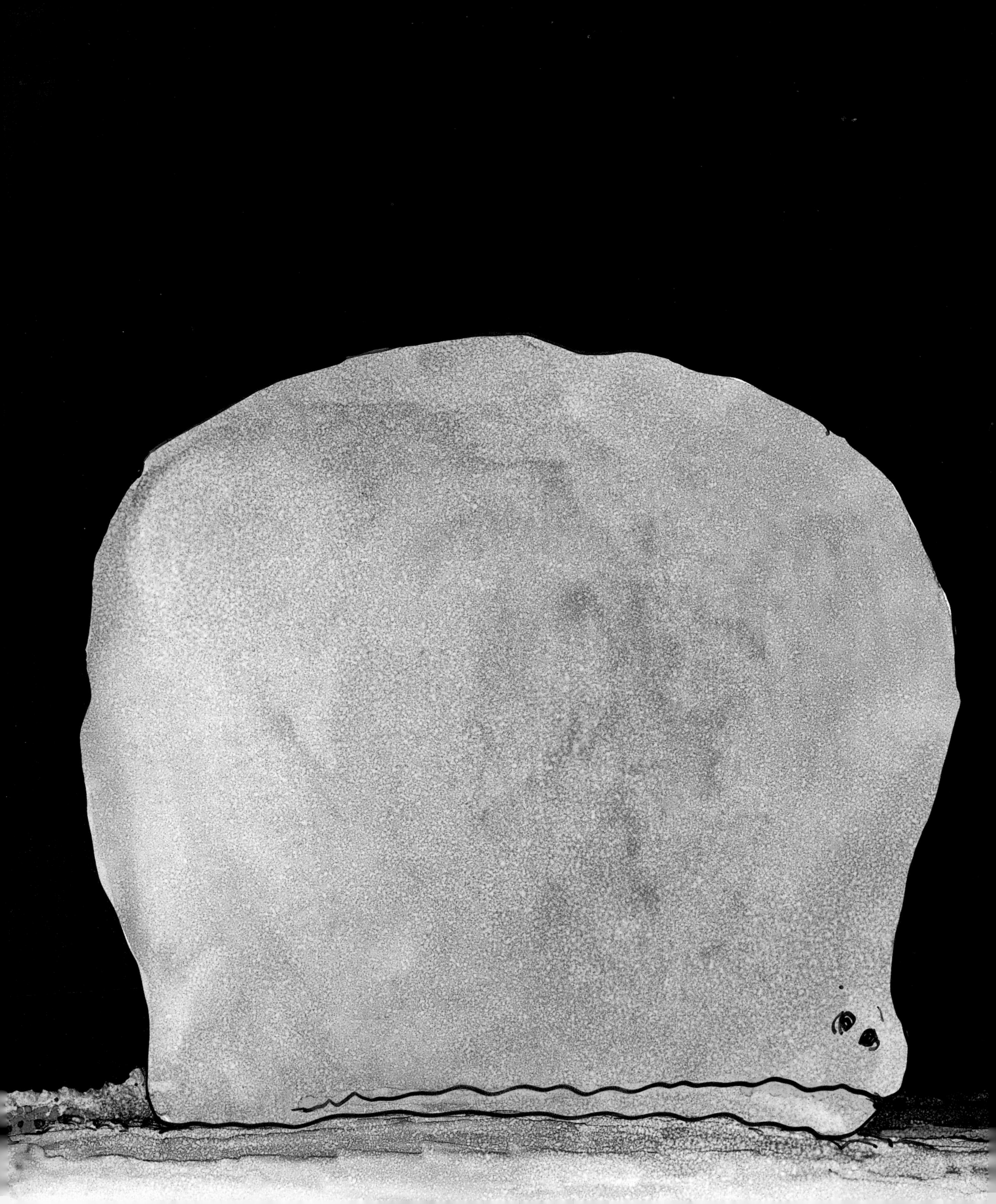

The cow was big and fat and slowed the GLERP down. And oh, how sick the GLERP did feel. "Sick or not I must go on walking," he said.

Just then an elephant came by.

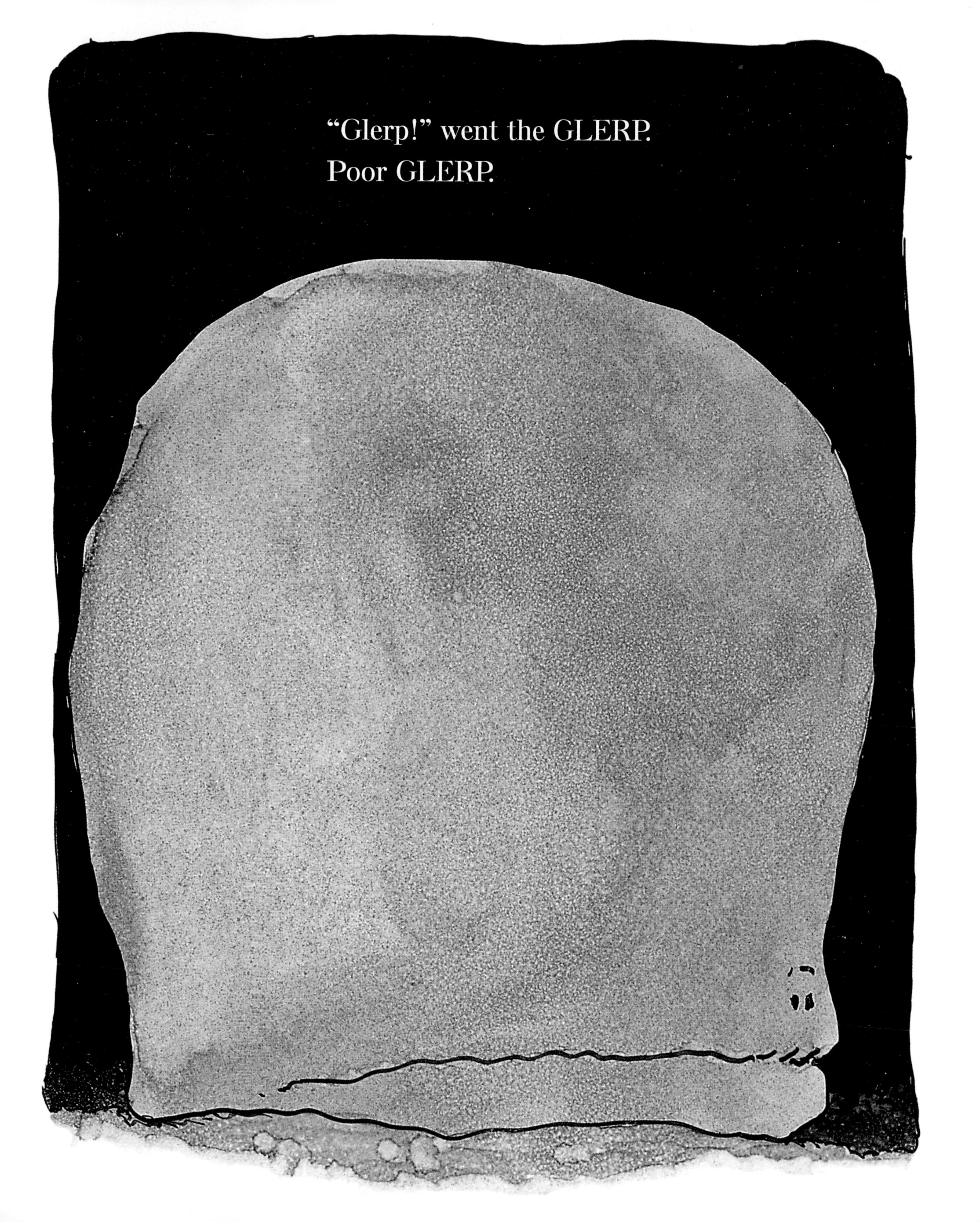

"Glerp!" went the GLERP.
Poor GLERP.

The elephant's tusks got stuck in the GLERP'S throat and he coughed and he coughed and he coughed and he coughed.

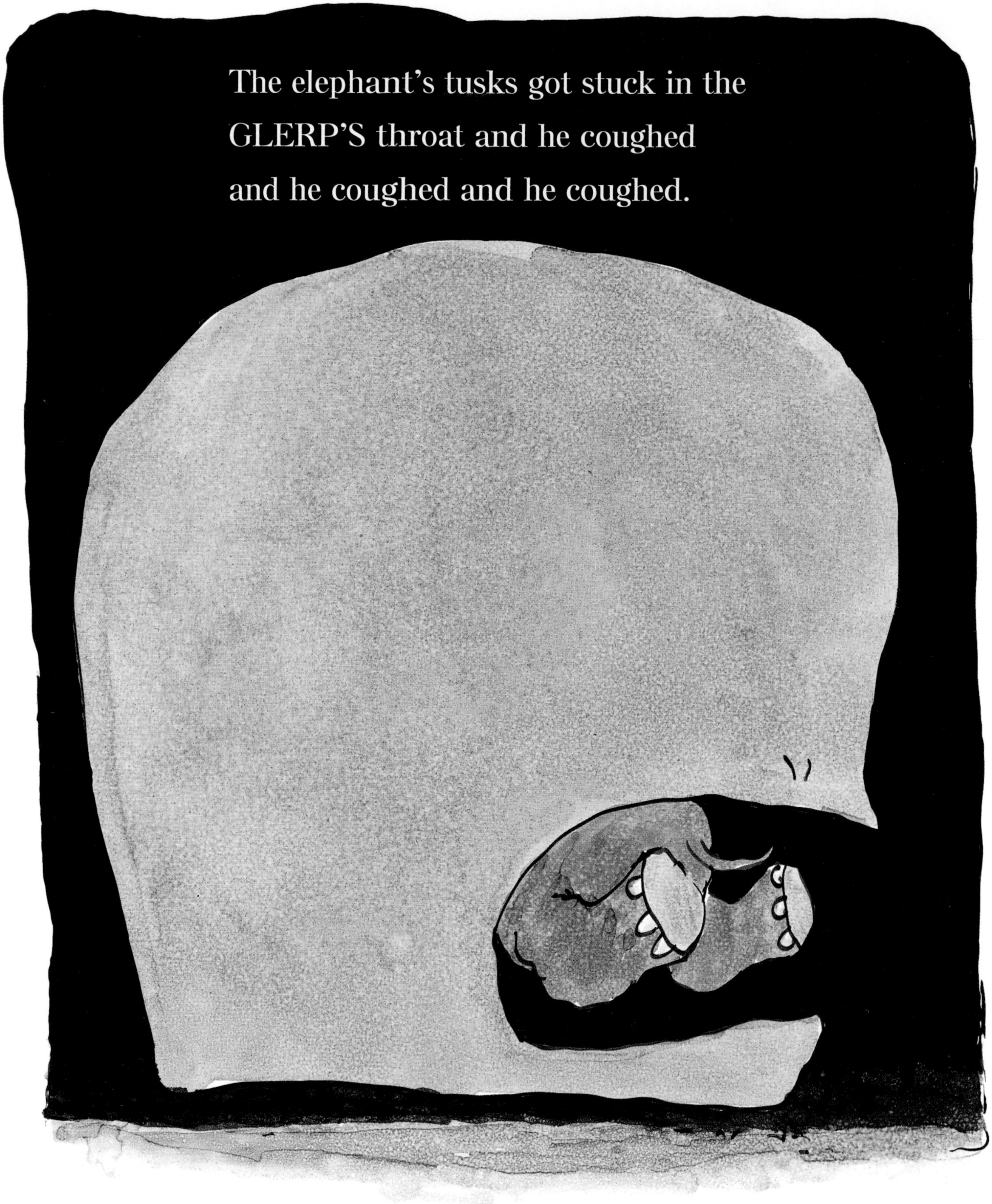

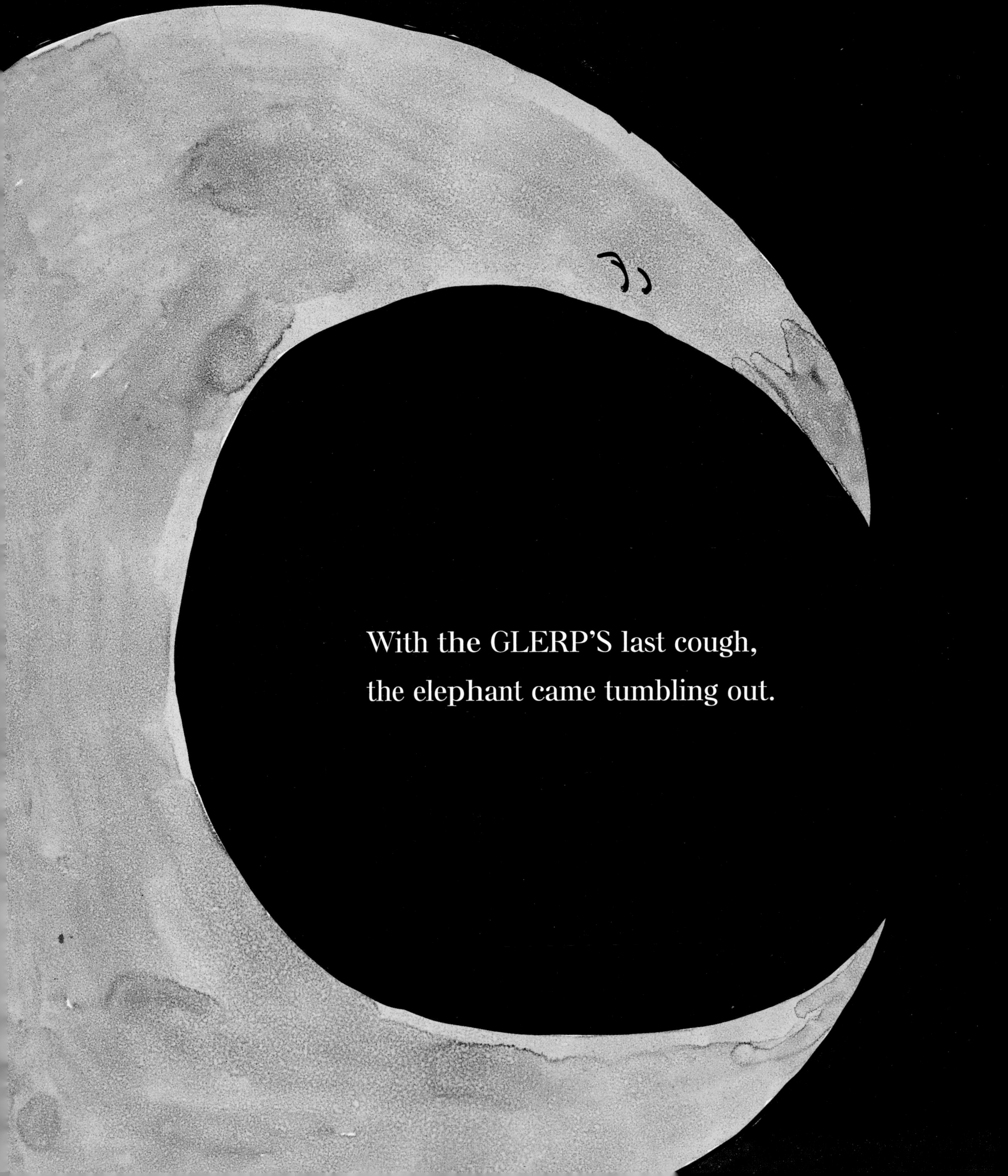

With the GLERP'S last cough,
the elephant came tumbling out.

Then out came the cow, the lion, the dog, the mouse, and last of all the ant.

"Oh, thank you, good fellow," they said to the GLERP. "We had a wonderful ride. When you are well, can we do it again?"

POOR GLERP.